A catalogue record for this book is available from the British Library

Published by Ladybird Books Ltd
80 Strand, London, WC2R 0RL
A Penguin Company

2 4 6 8 10 9 7 5 3 1
© LADYBIRD BOOKS LTD MMVIII
LADYBIRD and the device of a Ladybird are trademarks of Ladybird Books Ltd

ISBN: 978-1-84646-926-8

Printed in China

My Storytime

Don't Worry, Henry Puppy

written by Ronne Randall
illustrated by Simona Dimitri

Henry Puppy and Sam Bunny were
best friends. Every day they played tag,
chase-the-ball, who-can-jump-higher
and hide-and-seek. They had so much
fun together!

Then one day Sam moved away to a new home.

Henry was sad. He missed his friend.

But then Henry realised that he could go to visit Sam! As Sam's new home was far away, Henry made up a special rhyme to help him remember how to get there.

"Along the lane and past the mill,
Turn right at the big tree, go over the hill."

"Past the field where the horses play –
I'm off to see Sam and I know the way!"

Sam was always happy to see his friend. And Henry was happy to be there. But sometimes he felt a little worried.

"What if I forget the way next time I come?" he asked Sam. "Or what if I get lost going home?"

"You don't need to worry," Sam told him.
"If you get lost, just go back the way you
came! All you have to do is think of this
special rhyme:
"*If you lose your way,*
Don't be downhearted.
Just follow your steps
Back to where you started!"

One night, there was a loud and blustery storm. The wind howled and moaned and shook the branches of the trees. Henry couldn't sleep.

"I hope I'll be able to visit Sam tomorrow," he thought.

By the next morning the storm was over. The air was calm and clear, and the sun was shining.

"I *will* be able to visit Sam today," thought Henry happily.

As he set off, Henry noticed big heaps of leaves in the lane. "The storm must have blown them from the trees last night," he thought.

Henry jumped and danced through the leaves. "This is fun!" he laughed, kicking them high into the air.

As he went along, Henry said his rhyme to himself.

*"Along the lane and past the mill,
Turn right at the big tree, go over the hill."*

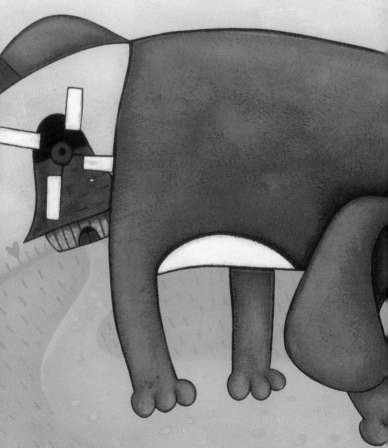

He ran along the lane as he always did, and scurried past the mill.

Suddenly Henry stopped. Where was the big tree? He couldn't see it anywhere! Henry was so confused that he didn't know which way to turn.

He ran down the lane, trying to remember the rest of the way to Sam's house.

"Past the fields where the horses play," he said to himself. *"I'm off to see Sam and I know the way!"*

But Henry didn't see the field where the friendly horses played. Instead he saw an old barn and some chickens.

"I can't remember seeing *this* on the way to Sam's house," he thought as he passed by.

Henry went on, and after a while he came to a field.

"This must be where the horses play!" he said to himself. But it wasn't. There were no horses in this field, just a raggedy old scarecrow.

"I can't remember seeing this on the way to Sam's house!" said Henry. He was very worried now. In fact, he felt like crying.

Then Henry remembered the rhyme Sam
had taught him.

"If you lose your way,
Don't be downhearted.
Just follow your steps
Back to where you started!"

"That's what I need to do," thought Henry.
"I'll go back the way I came!"

Back Henry went, past the scarecrow...
past the old barn... and past the chickens.

23

At last Henry found himself back at the
bottom of the hill.

"I know where I am now," he said.
"And there's the big tree. It must have
blown over in the storm last night!"

Henry leapt over the tree trunk, and scampered merrily down the lane. Before he knew it he could see his friends, the horses. "Here's the field where the horses play," he said. *"I'm off to see Sam and I know the way!"*

And so little Henry found his way to Sam's home at last.

"Oh, I'm so glad to see you!" Sam exclaimed. "I was worried. I thought you might have got lost!"

"I *did* get lost," said Henry.

"Then how did you get here?" asked Sam.

"I did exactly what you told me to," said Henry. "Although I was lost, I wasn't downhearted – I just followed my steps back to where I started! And now I'll never worry about getting lost again!"

And off they went for a lively game of chase-the-ball.